Marisol McDonald Doesn't Match
Marisol McDonald no combina

Story / Cuento
Monica Brown

Illustrations / Ilustraciones
Sara Palacios

Spanish translation / Traducción al español
Adriana Domínguez

Children's Book Press ◉ an imprint of Lee & Low Books Inc.
New York

My name is Marisol McDonald, and I don't
match. At least, that's what everyone tells me.

Me llamo Marisol McDonald y no combino.
Al menos eso es lo que me dicen todos.

I play soccer with my cousin Tato and he says, "Marisol, your skin is brown like mine, but your hair is the color of carrots. You don't match!"

"Actually, my hair is the color of fire," I say and kick the ball over Tato's head and into the goal.

Cuando juego al fútbol con mi primo Tato él me dice:

—Marisol, tu piel es morena como la mía, pero tu pelo es del color de las zanahorias. ¡No combinas!

—En realidad, mi pelo es del color del fuego—le contesto pateando la pelota, que vuela sobre su cabeza, llegando al arco.

My brother says, "Marisol, those pants don't match that shirt! They clash."

But I love green polka dots and purple stripes. I think they go great together. Don't you?

Mi hermano dice:

—Marisol, esos pantalones no combinan con esa blusa. ¡Chocan!

Pero a mí me encantan los lunares verdes y las rayas moradas. Creo que van muy bien juntos. ¿No crees?

I also love peanut butter and jelly burritos, and speaking Spanish, English, and sometimes both.

"Can I have a puppy? A furry, sweet *perrito*?" I ask my parents. "*¿Por favor?*"

"*Quizás,*" Mami says.

"Maybe," Dad says, smiling and winking.

También me encantan los burritos de mantequilla de maní y jalea, y hablar español e inglés, a veces al mismo tiempo.

—¿Puedo tener un perrito? ¿Un *puppy* dulce y peludito?—le pido a mis padres—. *Please*?

—Quizás—dice mami.

—*Maybe*—dice Dad sonriendo y guiñando.

My teacher, Ms. Apple, doesn't like the way I sign my name. "Marisol McDonald," she says, "this doesn't match! At school we learn to print and use cursive, but not at the same time."

But I like the way *Marisol McDonald* looks.

A mi maestra, la Srta. Apple, no le gusta cómo firmo mi nombre.

—Marisol McDonald—dice—¡esto no combina! En la escuela aprendemos a escribir en letra de imprenta y en cursiva, pero no a usarlas a la misma vez.

Pero a mí me gusta cómo luce *Marisol McDonald* cuando lo escribo.

At recess, Ollie and Emma want to play pirates, and Noah wants to play soccer.

"How about soccer-playing pirates?" I suggest.

"No way!" they say, so I run off to play on the swings by myself.

En el recreo, Ollie y Emma quieren jugar a los piratas, pero Noah quiere jugar al fútbol.

—¿Por qué no jugamos a los piratas futbolistas?—les sugiero.

—¡Porque no!—contestan, y me voy corriendo a los columpios a jugar sola.

After recess, we have art—my favorite subject.
I think my drawings surprise my friends.

Después del recreo tenemos la clase de arte, mi favorita.
Creo que mis dibujos sorprenden a mis amigos.

At lunch, Ollie walks over to me and scrunches his nose.

"A peanut butter and jelly burrito?" he asks.

"I know, I know," I say, "it doesn't match. But it sure tastes good."

"Marisol, you couldn't match if you wanted to!" Ollie says.

"Oh yeah? I bet I can!"

A la hora del almuerzo, Ollie se me acerca arrugando la nariz.

—¿Un burrito de mantequilla de maní y jalea?—pregunta.

—Ya sé, ya sé—le contesto—no combina. ¡Pero es delicioso!

—Marisol, ¡tú no podrías combinar aunque trataras!—dice Ollie.

—¿Ah sí!? ¡Te apuesto a que sí puedo!

The next day I wake up and decide that today I, Marisol McDonald, will match.

It's a little hard to find clothes that are all the same color.

Cuando me despierto al día siguiente decido
que hoy, Marisol McDonald va a combinar.

No es fácil encontrar ropa del mismo color.

I play pirates with Ollie at recess, but it's not very fun. Why can't pirates play soccer, anyway?

I have a regular peanut butter and jelly sandwich at lunch and the bread tastes. . .mushy.

Juego a los piratas con Ollie en el recreo, pero no me divierto mucho. ¿Por qué no pueden jugar al fútbol los piratas?

Como un sándwich de mantequilla de maní y jalea a la hora del almuerzo, pero el pan sabe... blando.

de sumar una
monio con la expo
de una lona que dice
casar conmigo?"
Hotel Quinto Sol: Hidalgo 26
Purificación, San Juan Teoti
Estado de México / Lu a Do
horas / $1900 por persona
compartido; $2500 por pe
AEROSTÁTICO NACIONAL
ñías de Tequisquiapan, con vista
golf, las minas de ópalo y los past
zales y sembradíos. Hay paquete
A 20 kilómetros d
Se toma la c
parte de
el vuelo con
prefieres, tomar
erte un master de

Even art class is a little bit boring.

"Marisol," Ms. Apple says, "What's wrong?
This doesn't look like your usual work."

"I'm trying to match," I say with a frown.

"Why?" asks Ms. Apple.

I can't think of a single good reason.

Hasta la clase de arte me aburre un poco.

—Marisol, ¿qué sucede? Este no se parece a tus trabajos usuales—dice la Srta. Apple.

—Estoy tratando de combinar—le contesto frunciendo el ceño.

—¿Por qué?—pregunta la Srta. Apple.

No se me ocurre una buena razón.

23

At the end of the day, Ms. Apple hands me a note.
I open it and it says:

Marisol,

I want you to know that I like you just the way you are,
because the Marisol McDonald that I know is a creative,
unique, bilingual, Peruvian-Scottish-American, soccer-playing
artist and simply marvelous!

    Ms. Jamiko Apple

                  I skip all the way home.

Al final del día, la Srta. Apple me da una nota.
La abro y la leo:

Marisol:

Quiero que sepas que te aprecio tal y cómo eres, porque
la Marisol McDonald que conozco es una artista y
jugadora de fútbol peruana-escocesa-estadounidense,
bilingüe, creativa, única ¡y simplemente maravillosa!

Srta. Jamiko Apple

Brinco todo el camino a casa.

When I wake up on Saturday I put on my pink shirt, my polka dot skirt, and my favorite hat—the one my *abuelita* brought me from Peru.

At breakfast I say, "My name is Marisol McDonald and I don't match because...I don't want to!"

"Bravo!" says Mami.

"Good for you," says Dad. "Now let's go to the pound and get a puppy!"

Cuando me despierto el sábado me pongo mi camisa rosada con mi falda de lunares y mi sombrero favorito, el que mi abuelita me trajo de Perú.

Durante el desayuno digo: —Me llamo Marisol McDonald y no combino porque... ¡no quiero hacerlo!

—¡Bravo!—dice mami.

—Me alegro por ti—dice Dad—. Ahora, ¡vamos a la perrera a buscar tu perrito!

When we get to the pound, there are big dogs and little dogs. There are dogs with long noses and dogs with smushed faces. There are chocolate colored puppies and smoky gray puppies and puppies the color of caramel.

How will I ever choose?

Cuando llegamos a la perrera, vemos perros grandes y perros pequeños. Hay perros con hocicos largos y perros con caras chatas. Hay perritos del color del chocolate, perritos color gris humo y perritos color caramelo.

¿Cómo escogeré el mío?

Then I see him. He has one floppy ear and one pointy ear, one blue eye and one brown eye. He is beautiful!

I walk over and he leaps into my lap. I cuddle him and it sounds like he purrs.

"I think we found just the right dog for you, Marisol," Mami says.

My puppy is perfect. He's *mismatched* and simply marvelous, just like me. I think I'll name him. . .

Kitty!

Hasta que lo veo: Tiene una oreja caída y una puntiaguda; un ojo azul y uno café. ¡Es hermoso!

Camino hacia él y salta en mi falda. Lo abrazo y parece que ronroneara.

—¡Creo que hemos encontrado el perro perfecto para ti, Marisol!—dice mami.

Mi perrito es perfecto. Él *no combina* y es simplemente maravilloso, igual que yo. Creo que lo llamaré...

¡Minino!

I wrote this book because, like more than six million Americans, I'm multiracial. I'm the daughter of a South American mother and a North American father, and my childhood was spent in a close community of cousins, *tíos*, and *tías*.

Like Marisol McDonald, my cousins and I are mixed—indigenous Peruvian and Spanish mixed with Scottish and Italian and Jewish, not to mention Nicaraguan, Mexican, Chilean and African. One thing most of us do share, are freckles. According to one of my *tíos*, the family freckles came from the time my *abuelita* was stirring a big pan of chocolate on the stove—my *tío* reached for it and it splattered everywhere, leaving chocolate sprinkles on everyone's faces and toes!

People sometimes ask us, "What are you?" and sometimes even say that we "don't match." But we know better. Our mothers told us that we are Americans, yes, but also citizens of the world. My life (and I'll bet yours too) is bound up with the history of many peoples, and like Marisol McDonald, I open my arms wide and embrace them all.

—Monica Brown

Monica Brown is the author of award-winning bilingual books for children. Her books are inspired by her Peruvian American heritage and a desire to share Latino/a stories with children. Monica is a Professor of English at Northern Arizona University, specializing in U.S. Latino Literature and Multicultural Literature. She lives with her husband and two daughters in Flagstaff, Arizona.
For my darling Juliana, your sweetness makes my every day. —M.B.

Sara Palacios was born and raised in Mexico City. She holds degrees in Graphic Design, Illustration, and Digital Graphic Techniques from universities in Mexico, and is pursuing her MFA in Illustration at the Academy of Art University in San Francisco. She has worked as a freelance illustrator for Santillana, McGraw-Hill, SM, Children's Book Press, and others.
To Ylda and Esau (Mom and Dad) who have always, always supported my decisions and have learned to embrace my mismatches. Because we don't have to be like everyone else or follow their paths. Our own choices make us who we are. —S.P.

A note on the translation: The title of this book presented a dilemma—how to translate the phrase "Marisol McDonald doesn't match" into Spanish? Even in English, a person can't "not match"—only two *things* (or colors, or qualities) can't match. In Spanish, there are many different verbs that mean "to match," but they present the same problem that they do in English—they sound a little funny applied to a person instead of two objects. Ultimately, we decided that the Spanish verb that most closely matched the sense of the English was *combinar*. We think Marisol herself would approve. —The Editor

Text copyright © 2011 by Monica Brown
Illustrations copyright © 2011 by Sara Palacios
Spanish translation by Adriana Domínguez

Children's Book Press, an imprint of
LEE & LOW BOOKS Inc., 95 Madison
Avenue, New York, NY 10016
leeandlow.com

Manufactured in China by Regent Publishing Services, July 2013
Book design by Carl Angel
Book production by The Kids at Our House
The text is set in Cscala
The illustrations are rendered in mixed media

10 9 8 7 6 5 4
First Edition

Library of Congress
Cataloging-in-Publication Data
Brown, Monica, 1969-
  Marisol McDonald doesn't match / story, Monica Brown; illustrations, Sara Palacios = Marisol McDonald no combina / cuento, Monica Brown; ilustraciones, Sara Palacios.
   p. cm.
  Summary: A creative, unique, bilingual, Peruvian-Scottish-American-soccer-playing artist celebrates her individuality.
  ISBN 978-0-89239-235-3
[1. Individuality–Fiction. 2. Racially mixed people–Fiction. 3. Hispanic Americans–Fiction. 4. Spanish language materials–Bilingual materials.] I. Palacios, Sara, ill. II. Title. III. Title: Marisol McDonald does not match. IV. Title: Marisol McDonald no combina.
PZ73.B68564 2011
[E]–dc23   2011012713

Special thanks to Citlali Tolia, Freda Mosquera, Imelda Cruz, Janet del Mundo, and Rod Lowe.